P9-DHL-019

Dear Parents,

Our world is filled with letters—those magical squiggles and lines we see on signs, in books, almost everywhere we look. Helping your child unlock the mystery of these squiggles can get him or her on the right track to reading success.

One way to lay the foundation for early reading success is reading to and with your child every day. **Step into Reading Phonics** books offer a unique way to turn daily reading into a pleasant and valuable experience. These books are designed to help your child learn about the sounds that letters stand for, how letters come together to make words, and how words can be put together to make sentences. They contain controlled text that introduces children to words they will see often in early reading books. Engaging illustrations help your child see the connection between words and pictures.

Begin by reading this book aloud to your child. As you read:

- Point to each word. This "tracking" of the print will help your child make a connection between the written and spoken word.
- Emphasize the sounds in rhyming words, such as *cat* and *hat,* or words that share a common consonant, such as *sand* and *silly.*
- Talk about the pictures on each page. Then say a word from the text and have your child find it. You can give hints, such as "This word starts with the /s/ sound" or "It rhymes with *cat.*"

When your child feels comfortable with the story, have him or her read it to you, a friend, or even a pet! Praise your child's efforts and encourage rereading of the story. Invite your child to find words from the story on signs or in other books. This will generate excitement about and interest in words.

Remember—all children deserve the gift of reading. As parents, you can help bestow that gift. Whatever you do, have fun with this book and instill the joy of reading in your child. It is one of the most important things you can do!

Wiley Blevins, Author and Reading Specialist
Ed.M., Harvard University

To our parents, our first teachers,
and to B.R.H., my soul mate
—K.E.H.

To Norby, with love
—D.K.H.

Text copyright © 2002 by Kathryn Heling and Deborah Hembrook.
Illustrations copyright © 2002 by Patrick Joseph.
All rights reserved under International and Pan-American Copyright Conventions.
Published in the United States by Random House Children's Books, a division of
Random House, Inc., New York, and simultaneously in Canada by Random House
of Canada Limited, Toronto.

www.randomhouse.com/kids

Library of Congress Cataloging-in-Publication Data
Heling, Kathryn.
Mouse makes magic / by Kathryn Heling and Deborah Hembrook ;
illustrated by Patrick Joseph.
p. cm. — (Step into reading. Step 1 book.)
SUMMARY: By changing their middle vowels, Mouse magically transforms
words into totally new ones.
ISBN 0-375-82184-8 (trade) — ISBN 0-375-92184-2 (lib. bdg.)
[1. Vocabulary—Fiction. 2. Mice—Fiction.] I. Hembrook, Deborah.
II. Joseph, Patrick, 1961– ill. III. Title. IV. Series.

PZ7.H37413 Mo 2002
[E]—dc21
2001048532

Printed in the United States of America   First Edition   August 2002   10 9 8 7 6 5 4 3 2 1

STEP INTO READING, RANDOM HOUSE, and the Random House colophon are registered
trademarks of Random House, Inc.

Step into Reading®

MOUSE MAKES MAGIC

A Phonics
Reader

A Step 1 Phonics Book

by Kathryn Heling & Deborah Hembrook
illustrated by Patrick Joseph

Random House 🏠 New York

Mouse is magic,
Mouse is quick.

Changing letters
is his trick.

Mouse finds words
and makes them new—
with magic vowels
a, e, i, o, u.

A pig is in a pen.
Mouse waves his
magic wand.

When the e
becomes an a,
the pig is in a pan!

A squirrel bites a nut.
Mouse waves his
magic wand.

net

When the u
becomes an e,
the squirrel bites a net!

A book is on Sam's lap.
Mouse waves his
magic wand.

When the a
becomes an i,
the book is on
Sam's lip!

A girl hops on one leg.
Mouse waves his
magic wand.

When the e
becomes an o,
the girl hops on
one log!

hat

A lady wears a hat.
Mouse waves his
magic wand.

hut

When the a
becomes a u,
the lady wears a hut!

A fish flaps her fin.
Mouse waves his
magic wand.

fan

When the i
becomes an a,
the fish flaps her fan!

Grandma holds a bud.
Mouse waves his
magic wand.

bud

When the u
becomes an e,
Grandma holds a bed!

sax

A man plays a sax.
Mouse waves his
magic wand.

When the a
becomes an i,
the man plays a six!

cub

A bear hugs her cub.
Mouse waves his
magic wand.

When the u
becomes an o,
the bear hugs her cob!

A man drives a rig.
Mouse waves his
magic wand.

rug

When the i
becomes a u,
the man drives a rug!

A man pushes a mop.
Mouse waves his
magic wand.

When the o
becomes an a,
the man pushes a map!

Mouse is magic.
He thinks it is fun
to play his tricks,
but now he is done.

zip
zap

bag
bog

pit
pot

rat
rot

set
sit

tax
tux

You can do
this magic, too!
Just change the vowel
to make words new!